Library and Archives Canada Cataloguing in Publication

Title: Phoenix gets greater / written by Marty Wilson-Trudeau with Phoenix Wilson ; illustrated by
    Megan Kyak-Monteith.
Names: Wilson-Trudeau, Marty, author. | Wilson, Phoenix, author. | Kyak-Monteith, Megan,
    illustrator.
Identifiers: Canadiana (print) 20220203865 | Canadiana (ebook) 2022020389X | ISBN
    9781772602531 (hardcover) | ISBN 9781772603040 (softcover) | ISBN 9781772602548 (EPUB)
Subjects: LCGFT: Picture books.
Classification: LCC PS8645.I4748 P46 2022 | DDC jC813/.6—dc23

Editor: Jazz Cook
Printed and bound in Canada

*Second Story Press gratefully acknowledges the support of the Ontario Arts Council and the Canada
Council for the Arts for our publishing program. We acknowledge the financial support of the
Government of Canada through the Canada Book Fund.*

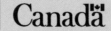

Published by
Second Story Press
20 Maud Street, Suite 401
Toronto, Ontario, Canada
M5V 2M5
www.secondstorypress.ca

"*Phoenix Gets Greater* is a timely and necessary addition to our collective Two-Spirit stories! Its
collaboration between mother and son, its engrossing color palettes that reflect Anishinaabe
acceptance and wholeness, and its charming, swirling protagonist make for a story that
should be shared with all of our children. Broaching the vast topic of Two-Spirit identities,
Marty Wilson-Trudeau and Phoenix Wilson have made a book I wish I had when I was a kid—
the wonders this book will do for our Indigenous and/or queer youth!"

—Joshua Whitehead, award-winning author of *Jonny Appleseed*

Phoenix Gets Greater

written by
Marty Wilson-Trudeau with Phoenix Wilson

illustrated by
Megan Kyak-Monteith

Second Story Press

When Phoenix was born, he was covered in very fine hair. His big brother called him 'Fuzzy' because he was fuzzy like a bear! Phoenix's mom and brother loved him very much.

But Phoenix was sick, and his doctors
said he would never be able to talk,
ride a bike, or kick a ball.

Phoenix's mom smudged him with the
four medicines: sage, tobacco, cedar, and
sweetgrass. She talked to the Creator
every day while Phoenix was in the hospital.

Slowly, Phoenix felt better!
He came home just in time for Halloween
and dressed up in a tiny pumpkin costume.

Phoenix found his mom's pink, fluffy blanket and took it with him everywhere. He rolled in it and dragged it around the house all day.

At the toy store, Phoenix loved to look at the dolls with all the pretty, colorful fabrics. He picked out soft, squishy dolls, fashion dolls, and dolls with long hair. As soon as he got home, he wrapped a towel on his head and pretended he had long hair too, swishing it all around.

Phoenix learned to spin, swish, and swirl so well
even his ballet teacher was impressed!

At Pow Wows, Phoenix twirled and twirled,
and the wool on his grass dance regalia twirled
with him.

But Phoenix loved shawl dancing best.
He put his fluffy blanket on his shoulders,
went up on his tiptoes, and danced like a
beautiful butterfly.

Phoenix didn't have friends who liked hockey, trucks, and bulldozers. He made friends with those who liked dolls and dancing too.

But sometimes, other kids made fun of Phoenix because he preferred dolls to trucks. They thought he was strange because he didn't act like the rest of the boys in their class.

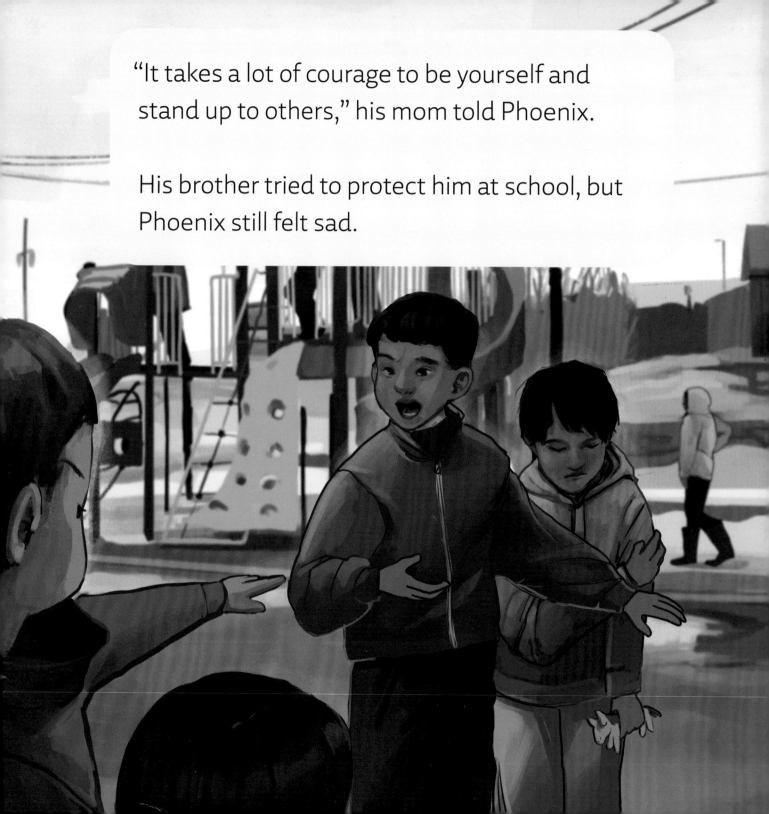

"It takes a lot of courage to be yourself and stand up to others," his mom told Phoenix.

His brother tried to protect him at school, but Phoenix still felt sad.

He stopped dancing and playing with his dolls. He even stopped twirling around his house.

One day, he sat down with his mom and brother. Crying, he told them, "I'm tired of hiding who I am. I'm not like the other boys in my class. I feel different. I am different."

Phoenix told his family he was gay. "I hope you won't stop loving me, and you'll accept me for who I am."

Phoenix's mom and brother pulled him close and started to cry too.

"We'll never stop loving you," Phoenix's mom said. "We love exactly who you are, and for that, you make us happy. I'm so proud of you."

"There's nothing wrong with being different," his brother comforted. "All that matters is that you're happy."

"We all carry a spirit within us," Phoenix's mom explained. "It gives us life and guides us. But in our Anishinaabe culture there are Two Spirit people, Niizh Manidoowag, who have both girl and boy spirits. Niizh is our word for two and manidoowag means spirit.

"That makes you extra special because
you think and feel like both boys and girls.
Anishinaabe communities have great respect
for Niizh Manidoowag. Their wisdom, healing
ways, and visions help our communities, and
they love to dance and twirl—just like you."

Phoenix started to smile. He couldn't believe it.
There were other people who were just like him!
And Niizh Manidoowag carried an important role in
his Anishinaabe culture, too.

The next day, he played with his dolls and laughed
as he swished and swirled in his pink, fluffy blanket.
The other kids' words didn't hurt so much anymore
because Phoenix was proud of being Two Spirit.

Now, Phoenix
has friends who
accept him for
all of who he is.

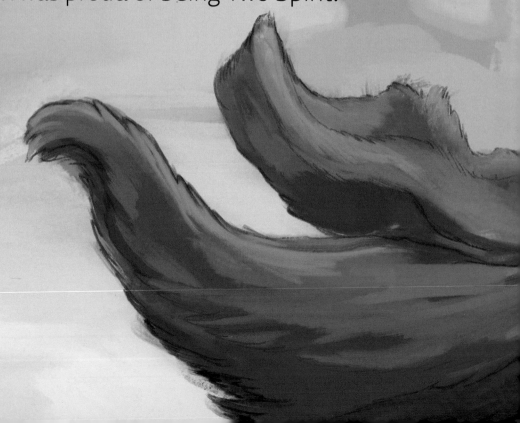

He still dances grass and shawl at Pow Wows—he twirls and swishes and swirls while his brother and mom cheer and clap!

Marty Wilson-Trudeau is an Anishinaabe Kwe writer originally from M'Chigeeng, Ontario, and a drama teacher at St. Charles College in Sudbury, Ontario. She is a mother to two wonderful sons, Brandan and Phoenix Wilson.

Phoenix Wilson is an Anishinaabe actor and dancer and is very proud of who he is. Phoenix started dancing ballet at age three, grass dancing at age five, and acting at age six. He can be seen in such projects as *Longmire*, *Letterkenny*, and the critically acclaimed movie *Wild Indian*. Phoenix is currently in Grade 11 where he excels in all his classes and has ambitions of becoming a corporate lawyer.

Megan Kyak-Monteith, from Pond Inlet, Nunavut, is an Inuk illustrator and painter. Graduating from NSCAD University in 2019, she currently lives and works in Halifax, Nova Scotia. In her illustrative projects, she works most often with Indigenous stories.

For my wonderful parents, Bill and Doris Wilson, who taught me the love of writing, and for Sadie Debassige, who loved me enough to let me go. This book would not be possible without the love and laughter from my two sons, Brandan and Phoenix. And to all LGBQT+ children and their families, you are not alone.

- M.W.T.

This book is dedicated to my best friend, my brother Brandan, and to my grandad, Bill, who even though he came from a different era always loved and accepted me. This is for every child out there who doesn't have the love and support from their families and peers. You were born this way.

- P.W.